29 DAYS OF SPIRITUAL GROWTH

Ashley Christie

29 DAYS OF SPIRITUAL GROWTH

Copyright © 2019 by Ashley Christie.

Published by: Ashley Christie

ashley.christie6@gmail.com

Editing & layout by: Tricia-Anne Y. Morris

tricianne.morris@gmail.com

Cover design by: Shenir Mcknight

ISBN: 978 976 8277 63 3

Presented to

....

....

By

....

....

Date

....

On the Occasion of

....

....

....

Contents

A c k n o w l e d g m e n t s

To all who have helped me along this journey, I express my sincere gratitude. This would not have been possible without your silent prayers and outward expression of encouragement!

Above all else, I acknowledge the head of my life, my Abba Father, who gave me the knowledge, wisdom and strength to complete this book.

Thank you All!
God bless You!

Preface

Writing this book was not at all easy. I am neither a reader nor a writer. So never in a million years would I have thought, I would be writing a book. If it was up to me, there would be no book but God had different plans.

The reality is it was a struggle to write. I could not decide whether to make it a devotional, a guide, or just a book that teaches and guide us as Christians. I later decided that the book would be one that teaches and guides us on how to get ready for Christ's return. However, when I started writing the manuscript, all hell broke loose. I had writer's block. I would lose my work every time I wrote a chapter. Every time I typed something, the last chapter I wrote went missing.

Eventually I gave up and went to God, "this is not my doing. I did not want to do this, so why are there so many issues. If this is you and this is your doing, then you'll have to be real clear on what you are requesting of me". That night as I went to bed, I had the most amazing experience in my dream.

I was around a table. Clouds surrounded me. I later saw a hand come through the clouds. I received a piece of paper. On the paper the words written were "Wait and see that I am God" (Malachi 3: 16). I was eager to get up and read more. As I read the passage in the morning. I realized that God had given me the confirmation to proceed. I did not know the passage. It was my first time seeing it. To sum it all up the passage spoke heavily about the day of judgement. Though I would not have thought of writing, I knew I had to be obedient to God.

The truth is, I have fallen many times along this Christian walk but I refuse to become rocky soil (Matthew 13:20-21). I refuse to let the problems and persecutions make me give up on living for Christ. I realize that I am not here to please people. The only applause I want to hear is that of my Heavenly Father. There is too much to gain. I refuse to lose it all. As long as there is life, I will keep moving towards Christ.

That is what I want for you too as you read these words. My desire is that each of you reading this will examine yourself and be prepared like Paul to change, wherever you need change. I pray after reading this you will get serious with me on this journey as we trample Satan's kingdom and build up the Kingdom of God.

Let us go make disciples and be on fire for God!

Ashley

D a y   1 ... C e r t a i n t y

"Let not your hearts be troubled. Believe in God; believe also in me. In my Father's house are many rooms. If it were not so, would I have told you that I go to prepare a place for you? And if I go and prepare a place for you, I will come again and will take you to myself, that where I am you may be also" (John 14:1-3)

The coming of the Lord is certain. Jesus promised his disciples that when everything was ready He would come for them. A similar account can be seen in Acts 1:11. As the disciples watched Jesus ascend into the clouds, two men in white apparel reminded them that the same Jesus they saw ascending into the Heaven would return in like manner.

If Jesus was wrong about the second coming, then we cannot trust anything else that He has taught us. The word of God says that God is not a man that he should lie (Numbers 23:19). To doubt that this grand event is certain is to doubt that God's Word (the Bible) is reliable and valid.

Having knowledge of the second return of Christ should not frighten us, but instead it should prepare us. It should help us to remain steadfast in our confidence that we will be with Him forever when He returns.

- *Action* -

Meditate on the Scripture below:

> *"Brothers and sisters, we do not want you to be uninformed about those who sleep in death, so that you do not grieve like the rest of mankind, who have no hope. For we believe that Jesus died and rose again, and so we believe that God will bring with Jesus those who have fallen asleep in him. According to the Lord's word, we tell you that we who are still alive, who are left until the coming of the Lord, will certainly not precede those who have fallen asleep. For the Lord himself will come down from heaven, with a loud*

2

command, with the voice of the archangel and with the trumpet call of God, and the dead in Christ will rise first. After that, we who are still alive and are left will be caught up together with them in the clouds to meet the Lord in the air. And so we will be with the Lord forever"

(1 Thessalonians 4:13-17)

Reflection:

What have you learnt from the passage above?

Notes

_____

_____

_____

_____

_____

_____

_____

_____

_____

_____

_____

_____

_____

_____

_____

_____

_____

_____

_____

_____

_____

_____

_____

_____

_____

Day 2 ... Unknown time

"But of that day and hour knoweth no man, no, not the angels of heaven, but my Father only" (Matthew 24:36)

The bible declares that no one but the Father knows the day of the second coming of the Lord. In fact, Paul's account in 1 Thessalonians 5:2 states that the Lord's return will be at an unexpected time like a thief in the night. The Bible however reveals several events to us that will occur before the Return of the Lord (Matthew 24: 4-29).

Having absolutely no knowledge of the day nor the time of the Lord's return means we should live in anticipation - we are to live our lives knowing that this event could happen at any time!

Paul states in 1 Thessalonians 5: 4-8, *"But ye, brethren, are not in darkness, that, that day should overtake you as a thief. Ye are all the children of light, and the children of the day: we are not of the night, nor of darkness. Therefore, let us not sleep, as do others; but let us watch and be sober. For they that sleep, sleep in the night; and they that be drunken are drunken in the night. But let us, who are of the day, be sober, putting on the breastplate of faith and love; and for an helmet, the hope of salvation."*

- *Personal Reflection* -

Read Matthew 24 in its entirety and write down the events listed. Now journal how you intend to live in anticipation of the Lord's Return.

Notes

_____

_____

_____

_____

_____

_____

_____

_____

_____

_____

_____

_____

_____

_____

_____

_____

_____

_____

_____

_____

_____

_____

Day 3 ... Stop and think

"I will send my messenger, who will prepare the way before me. Then suddenly the Lord you are seeking will come to His temple; the messenger of the covenant, whom you desire, will come, says the Lord Almighty. But who can endure the day of His coming? Who can stand when He appears?" (Malachi 3:1-2)

Have you ever stopped to think about Malachi 3 verses 1-2? The truth is some Christians believe after we have accepted Jesus as our Lord and Savior the journey ends there. We become complacent and our postures become that of persons merely waiting on the return of Jesus. We never stop to question how ready we are for His return. Perhaps it is because we think we have all the time in the world to live as we please.

The challenge is that this complacency causes us to lack full dedication to the things of God. We are not sold out to pursuing an intimate relationship with Him. We are just too happy to have escaped judgement and that is all that matters.

Paul tells us in 2 Corinthians 5:10 that there will come a time when we will all be judged before Christ, *"For we must all appear before the judgment seat of Christ; that every one may receive the things done in his body, according to that he hath done, whether it be good or bad"*. In other words, complacency is not an option for Christians. If we believe God requires change, then we must ask ourselves, **"Who can stand when He appears?"**

- Personal Reflection -

Do a recap of your life over the past year and ask yourself, "Have I been a complacent Christian?" If the answer is yes declare, "I will remain dedicated to the things of God and I will be a faithful servant. The devil will not steal what God has in store for me."

Notes

_____

_____

_____

_____

_____

_____

_____

_____

_____

_____

_____

_____

_____

_____

_____

_____

_____

_____

_____

_____

_____

_____

_____

_____

Day 4 ... Change differentiates the Saved from the unsaved

"This means that anyone who belongs to Christ is become a new person. The old Life is gone; a new life has begun" (2 Corinthians 5:17)

I am who I am and I will never change! Words that Christians sometimes use though I cannot fathom why. What does it mean when we say we cannot change and we claim to be the same even after accepting Christ as our Lord and Savior?

There was a man by the name of Saul. He had an encounter with Jesus on his way to Damascus. It changed his life forever. Before encountering Christ, Saul sought to kill the Lord's followers, causing great devastation among them. Saul changed once he met Christ. Saul whose name was changed to Paul became writer of the majority of the New Testament so through his work we could also seek to live blameless and pure lives until the return of Christ.

Paul admitted that he chose to forget his past and look toward his future. Paul knew an encounter with Christ required that he change from his old ways. He had to become a new creature.

Some Christians do not want to change. Perhaps because we have not yet grasped the reason for our call to accept Jesus as Lord and Savior to be a light unto the world reflecting His ways. I believe many of us are not living as children of God because our reason for walking with Christ has not become clear to us. This is why it is hard these days to differentiate the saved from the unsaved. In reality, some of us live as we please (by our own beliefs, ideas, principles and understanding, rather than God's).

Some Christians prefer the diluted, sugarcoated gospel because we find it easy to digest. We avoid the hardcore truth of the gospel of Christ. However, Paul contends in Philippians 3:19 that if we think only of this life and its pleasures we will miss out on the life that awaits us and this will lead to our destruction. C.S. Lewis puts it this way, "If you live for the next world, you get this one in the deal; but if you live only for this world, you lose them both."

- *Personal Reflection* -

Paul chose to forget the past. What are things from your past (old habits, norms, perspectives, attitudes etc.) that God wants you to forget in order to become more like Him?

Notes

_____

_____

_____

_____

_____

_____

_____

_____

_____

_____

_____

_____

_____

_____

_____

_____

_____

_____

_____

_____

_____

_____

_____

_____

_____

Day 5 ... The great deception

"For a time is coming when people will no longer listen to sound and wholesome teaching. They will follow their own desires and will look for teachers who will tell them whatever their itching ears want to hear"
(2 Timothy 4:3)

It seems that some Christians prefer prosperity and watered down messages. Now we have the hyper-grace movement. This movement has a cavalier attitude towards sin. It says once saved, we are always saved since we are saved by God's grace, which is everlasting. We know, however, that grace does not give us the right to sin (Romans 6:15). Rather it extends favor as God perfects us.

The law of God and the Grace of God are not at odds with each other. The law of God serves as a guide to our lives as Christians. The Bible speaks boldly on holiness and being set apart. This is why the Bible says, *"We know that God's children do not make a practice of sinning, for God's Son holds them securely, and the evil one cannot touch them"* (1 John 5:18). So let us not be deceived. Coming to Christ requires that we change. We must act as brand new creations. The old man should no longer have permission to occupy our lives.

If we are preparing for the heavenly place our Father has gone to prepare for us, how can we therefore deliberately sin against Him? How can we know His commands and disobey Him? People are watching us, and as a result may not come to Christ because of the way we live our lives. We live how we choose to, which makes it hard sometimes to separate the saints from the sinners. That is because some Christians talk like the world, act like the world, look like the world and do everything like the world. If we look and act no different what reason does that give the sinner to come to Christ? The Bible warns us about being obstacles to others, *"We put no obstacle in anyone's way, so that no one can discredit our ministry"* (2 Corinthians 6:3).

In these last days, we cannot afford to be deceived by anyone using the Gospel of Christ as an avenue to wealth or selfish gain. This will result in our destruction as Hosea says in chapter 4 verse 6,

"My people are destroyed for lack of knowledge: because thou hast rejected knowledge, I will also reject thee, that thou shalt be no priest to me: seeing thou hast forgotten the law of thy God, I will also forget thy children".

Eternity is at stake. This is serious business. It is time we get to the place where we make intentional steps towards doing what is pleasing in the sight of God. Remember, the heavenly Father to whom we pray has no favorites. He will judge or reward us based on what we do here on earth. We must live in reverent fear of Him during our time as *"foreigners in the land"* (Peter 1:17).

- *Personal Reflection* -

Are you being deceived by the modern day gospel and as a result a stumbling block to the unsaved? If yes, what are you going to do moving forward to help the unsaved come to know God?"

Notes

_____

_____

_____

_____

_____

_____

_____

_____

_____

_____

_____

_____

_____

_____

_____

_____

_____

_____

_____

_____

_____

_____

_____

_____

Day 6 ... Sweat like drops of blood

"And being in anguish, he prayed more earnestly, and
his sweat was like drops of blood falling to the ground"
(Luke 22:44)

One of the amazing things about the Bible is how it takes into consideration the saints and their faith. It also shows how much our flesh struggles. The best example of this took place in the Garden of Gethsemane. Jesus was in great agony when He realized that the hour of His death was almost near. He cried out to His Father because He did not want to have to endure the pain that was sure to come. In spite of this, He finally said to His Father, 'not My will but Yours'. Luke's account of this said Jesus was in such agony that sweat fell to the ground like great drops of blood.

What kept Jesus going? We were on His mind. He knew this was necessary so we would be given the chance to be with Him in Glory. Jesus knew that in order for us to have life, He had to lose His. He had great faith in His Father, He knew the pain was only for a moment and that after three days victory would be ours. The sweat in the form of blood drops was not enough to separate us from the reckless love of God, a love that leads to eternal life.

- Personal Reflection -

Take the next 15 minutes to reflect on Jesus' sacrifice for you. If He were before you now, what would you say?

Notes

_____

_____

_____

_____

_____

_____

_____

_____

_____

_____

_____

_____

_____

_____

_____

_____

_____

_____

_____

_____

_____

_____

_____

_____

_____

D a y   7 ... We   d i d n ' t   d e s e r v e   i t

"For God so loved the world that he gave his only begotten Son, that whosoever believeth in him should not perish, but have everlasting life" (John 3:16)

God showed the greatest love of all. While we were sinners, He sent His Son to die for us, even though we did not deserve it.

When we look back on our past and the things we have done, there are things we cannot share with others because we are ashamed of them. Yet God still chose us. Did we deserve it? No! Nevertheless, because of Jesus's obedience and love for His Father, because of God's sacrificial love, we have a chance at eternal life.

If God did this for us and we can see His goodness in our lives why do we walk around hating others? We go through life in malice, envy, jealousy, slander; void of Christ like love. What if for a second

God treated us the way we treat others? What if He took His love from us? Where would we be? As Christians, we need to do self-reflection. This calls for us to roll back the curtains of our lives to see where God has brought us from and to come to a place of understanding that real love is about loving the way God loves us, having compassion for others, and asking God for a heart of love even when others hurt us.

- *Personal Reflection* -

Paul describes love in 1 Corinthians 13. I charge you right now to mediate on the Scripture and look within yourself. If you identify an area where you are struggling, where you are not bearing the fruits of love, then ask God to give you a heart to love as 1 Corinthians 13 says you should.

Notes

_____

_____

_____

_____

_____

_____

_____

_____

_____

_____

_____

_____

_____

_____

_____

_____

_____

_____

_____

_____

_____

_____

_____

Day 8 ... A heart like His

"But while he was still a long way off, his father saw him and was filled with compassion for him; he ran to his son, threw his arms around him and kissed him"
(Luke 15:20)

One of my favorite parables in the bible is the story of the prodigal son (Luke 15:11-31). The parable directly shows the heart of God towards us, both sinners and saints alike. It highlights to us, how God rejoices over us whenever we come back to Him despite what we have done. It shows how forgiving and merciful God is towards us. Ultimately, the parable of the prodigal son proves there is nothing we can do to make God love us any less than He already does. His love leads to forgiveness.

Despite the number of times we disobey God and His Word, He forgives us. Despite the number of times God forgives us, we often find it hard to show the same level of love and forgiveness to others around us. I often ask, how can we be Christians and not love our enemies as ourselves? Notice I did not mention a loving family nor friendships since that part is easy. However, if we can love our enemies as ourselves we would have answered God's call to love everyone. We would show the world we are truly disciples of Jesus. If we have no love then how can we say we are children of God?

"A new command I give you: Love one another. As I have loved you, so you must love one another. By this all men will know that you are my disciples, if you love one another" (John 13:34-35).

- *Personal Reflection* -

Take a moment and reflect on how you treat others. Is it how God would want you to? If your answer is no ask God to stir up the spirit of love in you. (2 Timothy 1:7)

Notes

_____

_____

_____

_____

_____

_____

_____

_____

_____

_____

_____

_____

_____

_____

_____

_____

_____

_____

_____

_____

_____

_____

Day 9 ... Not in vain

"Let us not grow weary in well-doing, for in due time we will reap a harvest, if we do not give up" (Galatians 6:9)

How we love others reveals our love for God and one of the key things regarding loving others is to realize that what we are doing is not in vain as Paul stated in Galatians 6:9.

The truth is, if we cannot love the people around us, we cannot love God. John made it clear in 1 John 4: 20 that if we do not love as God loves us then we are liars and we are not children of God. If we are not children of God then the place He has gone to prepare will not be our home. If more and more we learn to love others even when it is hard to love them, then we live in God and living in God will perfect us daily!

Knowing that our lives are temporary should get us to act rightly at all times, no matter how hard things are. Loving others should bring us great joy, because the reality is, we are not living for those around us. Rather, we are living for the One with whom we shall spend eternity.

- *Action* -

Do you sometimes feel burdened to love others? If yes, say this prayer "Lord Jesus, help me to not feel burdened with loving others, even when loving them is hard. Instead, remind me daily that what I am doing is not in vain and that I will be rewarded for my good works here on this earth. In Jesus name I pray, Amen"

Meditate on the scripture below:

> *"But love your enemies, do good to them, and lend to them without expecting to get anything back. Then your reward will be great..."* (Luke 6:35)

Notes

_____

_____

_____

_____

_____

_____

_____

_____

_____

_____

_____

_____

_____

_____

_____

_____

_____

_____

_____

_____

_____

_____

Day 10 ... Love forgives even if forgiving is hard

"Hate stirs up trouble, but love forgives all offenses"
(Proverbs 10:12)

One of the greatest things about love is that forgiveness follows, and with forgiveness, there is great peace. Love where there is unforgiveness is not of God.

I go back to the parable of the Prodigal son. It was love that moved the Father with great compassion when he saw his son from a distance. It was love that led him to hug and kiss his son even though his son had squandered his wealth. What is surprising about this story is the attitude of the older brother. It upset him that his father threw a big party for his younger brother who had sinned against him.

This attitude represents some of us as Christians today. If someone we love has done us wrong, we would find it hard to forgive him or her. Some of us are even unforgiving towards those who have not directly affected us. The truth is many of us have the spirit of the Prodigal son's brother. While his father was forgiving, the brother who this had nothing to do with was unforgiving.

We may say it is hard to forgive someone that has done us wrong, but no matter how hard it is, it is necessary for entering the Kingdom of God. How can we want forgiveness from our Heavenly Father when we refuse to forgive others? Matthew 6: 14-15 reads, *"For if you forgive other people when they sin against you, your heavenly Father will also forgive you. But if you do not forgive others their sins, your Father will not forgive your sins".*

We must put pride aside and learn to forgive.

Does forgiving someone mean that what he or she has done to us is right? No, it does not mean that. It simply means we are releasing them into the hands of the Lord, and we are letting go of the anger, bitterness and resentment we have towards them. This is critical because the pain of unforgiveness can poison our souls. It can cause us to be devoid of peace. It is also critical because the action of forgiveness is an act of love. This is why we should make it our duty day and night, or whenever we pray to release those that have offended or hurt us, and ask God for a heart of love and compassion towards them (Mark 11:25).

Remember too, forgiveness does not equate to us being fools. It means we are protecting our peace, and we are walking how our Heavenly Father requires of us to walk. We must always ensure that we are doing what Christ requires. Even if we look like fools in the world's eyes. It is better to be a fool for Christ than to be a servant of the devil.

Forgiving others can be one of the hardest and greatest pains we experience in this life when we have been hurt by the ones we love. It can be heart wrenching. Nevertheless, Ephesians 4:31-32 says, *"Get rid of all bitterness, rage and anger, brawling and slander, along with every form of malice. Be kind and compassionate to one another, forgiving each other, just as in Christ God forgave you"*. It is not easy to do but we are preparing to go where our Father is, and as Christians, we know forgiveness is a requirement.

- Personal Reflection -

Take some time to reflect on the persons that have done you wrong. Think about how you feel towards them. What would your reaction be if you had to serve them the way the Prodigal son's brother had to serve him? Talk to God about your response.

Notes

_____

_____

_____

_____

_____

_____

_____

_____

_____

_____

_____

_____

_____

_____

_____

_____

_____

_____

_____

_____

_____

_____

_____

_____

Day 11 ... Forgiveness requires deliberate action

"Then Peter came up and said to him, "Lord, how often will my brother sin against me, and I forgive him? As many as seven times?" Jesus said to him, "I do not say to you seven times, but seventy-seven times"
(Matthew 18:21-22)

F orgiving others was one of the hardest things for me when I got saved. Persons I thought loved me had rejected me. I was privy to everything they said about me and because of that even when I came to Christ, loving others the way Christ wanted me to, was hard. I kept telling myself that they did not deserve my love. Then it finally dawned on me that God loves me, and I was a mess when He called me (I am still a mess at times) yet He still calls my name. "Though my sin was great, His love was greater".

I realized that despite what they had done I had to forgive them because God forgave me. I did not do it for them. I did it because God did it for me. I knew I had to be deliberate about forgiving those who had hurt or offended me. Therefore, I gave myself to studying God's love for me and prayed that I could come to a place where I would reciprocate this same love to others. I had to learn to see the best in people rather than constantly or automatically think the worst.

I had to remind myself daily that I am the light of the world, and that wherever I go I should light my candles for all to see (Matthew 5: 13-16). I had to remind myself daily that when people see me it must be obvious that being Christian means I cannot help but love and forgive as Jesus did and this had to be true even if people or scenarios hurt me repeatedly.

I also had to remind myself daily that God is my defender and my unforgiveness towards others prevents Him from working on my behalf in these difficult situations. God cannot defend that which opposes His principles. Like Nehemiah (chapter 4) I had to ignore my critics, be deliberate about forgiving them, then ask God to defend me.

- *Personal Reflection* -

Are you ready to make forgiving others a part of your daily prayer routine? Are you ready to move with compassion towards others that have done you wrong? If your answer is yes, whenever you are offended or hurt by others instead of responding out of anger, prayerfully ask God to give you the strength to fight against the discouragement. Also, remember the words in Matthew 5:7.

Matthew 5:7 "Blessed are the merciful, for they shall receive mercy".

Notes

_____

_____

_____

_____

_____

_____

_____

_____

_____

_____

_____

_____

_____

_____

_____

_____

_____

_____

_____

_____

_____

_____

_____

_____

Day 12 ... Twisted commands

"Now the serpent was more subtle than any beast of the field which the Lord God had made. And he said unto the woman, Yea, hath God said, Ye shall not eat of every tree of the garden?" (Genesis 3:1)

L ike Eve we face temptations daily. When we look at Genesis 3, the first record of temptation, we see that the devil tries to twist God's words. Notice what the serpent said to Eve *"Did God say you should not eat of any tree in the garden?"* The devil's words differed greatly from those spoken by God to Adam, *"You can eat of every tree, **except** the tree of the knowledge of good and evil"*. That is because the devil twisted God's words.

The devil often uses this tactic. He often has us believing 'it's just a little white lie'. He has us believing none of God's commands is as rigid as they seem. It is okay to not take them seriously. If we err, it is only a **'small sin'.** Those are all lies of the enemy. As Romans 6:23 says, *"For the wages of sin is death, but the gift of God is eternal life in Christ Jesus our Lord"*. In God's eyes, a sin is a sin, and He wants us to avoid sinning.

To avoid sinning we will each have to yield not to temptation. Note however that the temptation itself is not a sin, *"For we do not have a high priest who is unable to empathize with our weaknesses, but we have one who has been tempted in every way, just as we are - yet He did not sin"*. (Hebrews 4:15) Nevertheless, a temptation is not something to take lightly.

Temptation is the desire to sin, and that desire comes in many forms. The desire to pursue sexual immorality, lying, stealing, killing, cheating and the list goes on. Our goal ought to be to find godly ways to remain self-controlled, no matter how strong the temptations are.

- Personal Reflection -

Think about the last time you gave into temptation. What led you to fall and how will you deal with it next time?

Notes

_____

_____

_____

_____

_____

_____

_____

_____

_____

_____

_____

_____

_____

_____

_____

_____

_____

_____

_____

_____

_____

_____

Day 13 ... Magnetic attraction

"And when the woman saw that the tree was good for food, and that it was pleasant to the eyes, and a tree to be desired to make one wise, she took of the fruit thereof, and did eat, and gave also unto her husband with her; and he did eat" (Genesis 3:6)

D o you remember those little magnetic fruits or notepads that your parents or grandparents had on their refrigerator? Do you remember pulling it from the refrigerator and how strong the force was when you tried to put it back? Do you remember how it would attach itself without you having to be the one to stick it onto the surface of the refrigerator? This was because of the strong magnetic field. The magnetic field pulls iron and similar materials to itself. Temptation works in the same way. It is like a magnet.

Think of yourself as the magnet. The more you entertain ungodly things, the more they will pull themselves to you. The thing about temptation is that it seems enticing and fun at first, *"Eve saw that it was BEAUTIFUL"* (Genesis 3:6). However, the truth is the more you entertain it, the more desirable it will appear to you and then **BOOM** they trap you. Later the **guilt and shame** come, and the **consequences are never worth it.**

What is wonderful about our God though is the way He made the human mind. The human mind can never think about more than one thing at a time and our actions start with our thoughts (Matthew 15:18-19). The more we dwell on tempting situations the more appealing they become. If we shift our thoughts to something pure, noble and holy, the tempting thoughts will disappear.

- Action -

Use the passage below to help you whenever you are tempted to do something that is not Christ-like. Psalms 119:11 *"Your word have I hid in my heart that I might not sin against you."*

Notes

_____

_____

_____

_____

_____

_____

_____

_____

_____

_____

_____

_____

_____

_____

_____

_____

_____

_____

_____

_____

_____

_____

_____

Day 14 ... Submit to God, resist the devil and he will flee

"Submit to God. Resist the devil and he will flee. Draw nigh to God, and He will draw nigh to thee"
(James 4:7-8)

Temptations can be difficult to resist. You know what though. God has not left us helpless (1 Corinthians 10:13) and His promises are true. If we call on Him during tempting situations, He will give us a clear path of escape: *"Submit to God. Resist the devil and he will flee. Draw nigh to God, and He will draw nigh to thee"* (James 4:7-8).

One of the greatest stories about temptation was the one of Jesus in the wilderness for 40 days and

40 nights (Matthew 4:1-11). When we study this passage of Scripture it teaches us how as Christians to deal with temptation and the force behind it (the devil).

The devil started by tempting Jesus in the area He was presumably weakest. He commanded that Jesus turn the stones into bread because he knew after 40 days and nights Jesus would have been starving. **The bottom line** *is* the devil will tempt us in the area we struggle with the most.

- *Personal Reflection* -

What was Jesus's strategy when the enemy tempted Him? Have you made it a habit to use the Word of God as your weapon against temptation? Do you know the Word of God well enough to know what Scriptures to use as your defense when temptations face you?

Notes

_____
_____
_____
_____
_____
_____
_____
_____
_____
_____
_____
_____
_____
_____
_____
_____
_____
_____
_____
_____
_____
_____
_____
_____
_____

Day 15 ... The devil is not your friend

"Sin is crouching at the door, eager to control you. But you must subdue it and be its master" (Genesis 4:7)

L et us go back to the story in Matthew 4. The entire episode of Jesus in the wilderness reminds us of what God said to Cain in Genesis 4 verse 7. God has commanded us to be like Jesus, with the Word of God planted in our hearts so that once the devil comes one way, he flees several ways.

As believers preparing for the Kingdom of heaven, we must learn to abort the devil's tricks and plots before they come to full term. Satan is not our friend! In fact, he is a liar and his road leads to nothing but destruction. Because he is not our friend, we must have a warrior heart towards him. The attitude of Jesus in Matthew 4 is what we must emulate.

Jesus knew He had Kingdom business to take care of. Hence entertaining the devil was not even up for discussion. You and I are no different. We ought to realize that we are constantly at war with the enemy, and what we entertain we attract. We must realize that we have no time to play with fire, because if we play with it we will be burned (no pun intended). We cannot afford to have sin be our master. Remember eternity is at stake. We have a choice when it comes to temptation. We can choose to either entertain it or shut it down at its onset.

- Remember this -

The enemy is not your friend, but if you allow him, he can become your Master.

Notes

_____

_____

_____

_____

_____

_____

_____

_____

_____

_____

_____

_____

_____

_____

_____

_____

_____

_____

_____

_____

_____

_____

_____

Day 16 ... Not an easy road

"If you are guided by the Spirit, you won't obey your selfish desires" (Galatians 5:16)

E veryone struggles with temptation. As you master resisting one thing, another arises. How do I know this? Because I have been there and I still go through it.

I remember when I first received salvation. God told me not to watch my favorite TV show. Even though He said not to, I would try but could not watch the show in peace. I would constantly hear Him say, "This is not benefiting your spiritual life" and I would retort "But God why, it's just a show and I like it!" I often questioned His wisdom even though it was obvious He knew the seeds these shows would plant in my heart.

I was disobedient for a long time. Telling Him

I would be fine. My disobedience later led to nights where I had sexual thoughts. I felt disgusted. I' kept thinking, "Were the words written on my face, I would walk in shame".

God worked on me. No peace would come from watching the show. Suddenly, the show became boring. I completely lost interest. I no longer served two masters. I realized that old things had passed away and all things had become new (2 Corinthians 5:17). I was now a new Ashley, one who had to be about the works of her heavenly Father.

I grew obedient to the voice of God. I realized that if I did not guard my heart, then all kinds of ungodly seeds would be planted in my heart, and if I kept watering them, they would bloom. Today, I consciously take care in choosing what I listen to, watch, or entertain myself with. I have grown and I realize that I have a part to play in all of this. The Bible says, *"Submit to God, Resist the devil and he will flee, draw nigh to God and He will draw nigh to me"* (James 4:7-8). I now know if I do my part God will do His because God is not a man that He would lie (Numbers 23:19)! **His promises are true!**

My struggle may not be your struggle. Temptation comes in all shapes and forms. Anything that deviates from what God requires of you to do is a temptation. You must take note of the areas the devil attacks you in and work on them! Remember, it never ends until your life is over.

Also, be careful not to think you can do this on your own, that is useless (1 Corinthians 10:12). You need God every day to fight this! You must lift your eyes to the hills from whence cometh your help as your help comes from the Lord (Pslam 121:1). If you could do it by yourself the Bible would not read, *"I can do all things through Christ who strengthens me"*. Instead, it would read, "I can do all things through me, for I strengthen myself".

God has not left us without instructions. He has given us examples. He has shown us how to get out. What a good Father we have!

- Personal Reflection -

What is God telling you to let go of? Will you be obedient? Will you allow God to help you? **Remember eternity is at stake!**

Here are a few scriptures to help you. Make them a part of your life. Hide them in your heart.

✓ **Be on your guard.** *"Humble yourselves, therefore, under God's mighty hand, that He may lift you up in due time. Cast all your anxiety on him because He cares for you. Be alert and of sober mind. Your enemy the devil prowls around like a roaring lion looking for someone to devour"* (1 Peter 5:6-8).

✓ **Think Heavenly.** *"Finally, brothers and sisters, whatever is true, whatever is noble, whatever is right, whatever is pure, whatever is lovely, whatever is admirable—if anything is excellent or praiseworthy—think about such things. Whatever you have learned or received or heard from me or seen in me—put it into practice. And the God of peace will be with you"* (Philippians 4:8-9).

✓ **Pray to avoid Temptation.** *"Watch and pray so that you will not fall into temptation. The spirit is willing, but the flesh is weak"* (Matthew 26:41).

Notes

_____

_____

_____

_____

_____

_____

_____

_____

_____

_____

_____

_____

_____

_____

_____

_____

_____

_____

_____

_____

_____

_____

Day 17 ... Narrow way

"Narrow is the gate that leads to God's kingdom and it is difficult" (Matthew 7:13-14)

When we read the Matthew 7 passage, the word 'narrow' is significant. Narrow by definition means restricted or limited. For Christians, this means there is little space for us to do as we feel. God is not in the business of us negotiating with Him. Even though we try to do so sometimes, He has made it clear the road is narrow and our desire to please our flesh is not welcomed in His sight. He has set His commands and regardless of whether or not we like it, we signed up for His way when we accepted Jesus as our Lord and savior. The Christian path is a straight path.

Yes. Some of us may detour because the things of the world may sometimes be more pleasing to the eyes; things that may sometimes make us feel 'good'. This is what God is speaking of when He speaks of the broad road – the things of the world. However, the broad road leads to destruction. It has no limitations or restrictions regarding choice – good or bad. On the other hand, as Christians we do not have a choice. We cannot choose to obey what we want to obey and disobey what we deem to be displeasing.

- Personal Reflection -

On a scale of 1 to 10, where 1 means never and 10 means always, rate yourself on the three statements below. Scores below 7 may require that you repent and ask God to help you change in this area.

1. I obey God even when I don't understand why I need to
2. I obey God even when it's uncomfortable
3. I obey God even when I have my own ideas and plans

Notes

_____

_____

_____

_____

_____

_____

_____

_____

_____

_____

_____

_____

_____

_____

_____

_____

_____

_____

_____

_____

_____

Day 18 ... No more wishy-washy Christianity

"Do not love this world nor the things it offers you, for when you love the world, you do not have the love of the Father in you" (1 John 2:15)

L iving for Christ with an unshakable boldness can sometimes be challenging. We may feel like throwing in the towel because others around us are not living holy or righteous before God. People ask us to deny God and live like the world. Sometimes we even fall by the wayside giving into the pressures. There were three boys in the Bible (Shadrach Meshach, and Abednego) who refused to give in even when their lives were on the line. Though their punishment would be death for not participating in idol worship, they refused to be wishy-washy Christians.

In Daniel 3, King Nebuchadnezzar made a golden statue and called people from all races, nations and languages to bow to the ground at the sound of the musical instruments. They threw anyone who refused to bow and worship the statue into the blazing furnace. At the sound of the instruments Shadrach, Meshach, and Abednego refused to bow down. When Nebuchadnezzar heard he gave them one more chance to do so. Rather than bow and worship the statue, the three boys made this most profound statement:

"O Nebuchadnezzar, we do not need to defend ourselves before you. If we are thrown into the blazing furnace, the God whom we serve is able to save us. He will rescue us from your power, Your Majesty. But even if He doesn't, we want to make it clear to you, Your Majesty that we will never serve your gods or worship the gold statue you have set up". (Daniel 3:16-18)

Their answer proved that they were not in the business of compromising. They were determined to have faith in God even if He did not deliver them. They remind of us of the scripture *"Let your light so shine before men, that they may see your good works, and glorify your Father which is in heaven"* (Matthew 5:16).

They weighed the cost and counted the consequences of worshipping Nebuchadnezzar's statue. They did not want to deny God. For them there was no room for compromising for they knew that the end would be better than the beginning.

As children of God preparing to meet God in all His glory this is an attitude we ought to have. James said *"You adulterers! Don't you realize that friendship with the world makes you an enemy of God? I say it again: If you want to be a friend of the world, you make yourself an enemy of God"* (James 4:4). This means we cannot have one foot in and one foot out and believe that it is okay. We should not be living to please others but to please God. We have a standard to uphold. We cannot gamble it away for a moment of pleasure. It simply is not worth it.

God wants people who will stand up for Him. He wants people who will live for Him regardless of what the world throws at them. Joshua 24:14 says *"Choose this day who you will serve?"* We are either going to serve God intentionally or be friends of this world. **We cannot serve two masters.**

- *Personal Reflection* -

Spend some time and reflect on the Scripture below. Ask God to reveal to you how it applies to your life.

"Let there be no sexual immorality, impurity, or greed among you. Such sins have no place among God's people. Obscene stories, foolish talk and coarse jokes – these are not for you. Instead, let there be thankfulness to God.

You can be sure that no immoral, impure, greedy person will inherit the Kingdom of Christ and of God. For a greedy person is an idolater, worshipping the things of this world. Don't be fooled by those who try to excuse these sins, for the anger of God will fall on all who disobey him.

Don't participate in the things these people do. For once you were full of darkness, but now you have light from the Lord. So live as people of the light! For this light in you produces only what is good and right and true" (Ephesians 5: 3-9).

Notes

_____

_____

_____

_____

_____

_____

_____

_____

_____

_____

_____

_____

_____

_____

_____

_____

_____

_____

_____

_____

_____

_____

_____

_____

_____

_____

Day 19 ... Stand strong in the midst of change

"If we live, we live for the Lord; and if we die, we die for the Lord. So, whether we live or die, we belong to the Lord" (Romans 14:8)

P eople constantly say, "oh live a little", "enjoy your youth", "go to a little club now and then", "live life", "you only live once", "have sex if you want to, God will understand". Another popular one, "the Bible is ancient, things have changed and people have evolved. It is now the 21st century so get with the program". One thing I am certain of is that the Word of God has not changed. Times may have changed, culture may have changed, but God is the same yesterday, today and tomorrow.

I go back to the story of the three Jewish boys (Shadrach, Meshach, and Abednego). The culture had changed for them but they refused to change. They remained standing and God delivered them. They decided that conforming would not be an option.

Daniel had a similar resolve. It was illegal to pray. He prayed anyway. So what did God do? He delivered Daniel out of the lion's den just as He delivered the three boys from the blazing fire.

I hope you get the point! God rewards those who stand firm in Him and His Word. He will never leave us nor forsake us. And even if we die for what is right, we must count it as a gain because we know that standing for Christ, unwavering in the midst of changes in our culture, will bring us divine reward. We will have our reward, even if not here, in the place Jesus has gone to prepare for us.

- Action -

Prayer: Lord strengthen me so that when things around me change I will remain steadfast.

Notes

_____

_____

_____

_____

_____

_____

_____

_____

_____

_____

_____

_____

_____

_____

_____

_____

_____

_____

_____

_____

_____

Day 20 ... Faith

"And without faith it is impossible to please God,
because anyone who comes to him must believe that he
exists and that he rewards those who earnestly seek him"
(Hebrews 11:6)

W hen Abraham was tested by God to offer Isaac as a burned offering, he did not hesitate. He rose early, saddled his donkey then took Isaac and two servants with him. Abraham did as God commanded. Even more profound was how Abraham responded when Isaac asked him about the lamb. Abraham responded, **God will provide**.

Can you imagine God asking you to offer the child you have prayed for and waited on for so many years as a sacrifice? Few of us as Christians would respond as Abraham did. We would probably negotiate with God and go get a lamb to offer as sacrifice (lol! Do not get all holy on me). We would say get thee behind me Satan (Our famous saying when God's commands seem unrealistic).

I can only imagine the pain Abraham felt, but he made the sacrifice, anyway. Abraham understood that **Faith = Works**. Like Abraham, we must prove that we believe in God and His commands. We must make sacrifices too (time, desires, relationships and anything else God commands of us). James 2:14 reads, *"What good is it, dear brothers and sisters, if you say you have faith but don't show it by your actions? Can that kind of faith save anyone?"*

Even when we cannot see God's plan, we have to believe that greater will come of whatever sacrifice God commands of us. Our goal should be to 'Have faith and use our works to show whose we are and who our faith is in!'

- Personal Reflection -

Ask yourself, "Do my works reflect my faith in Jesus?" If no, it is time to change and use your works to reflect your faith. Say the prayer below:

Prayer: "Lord Jesus, your word says that if I don't show my faith in you by my works then that type of faith cannot save me! Lord, help me daily to use my works to match my faith in you and my hope in eternity."

Notes

_____

_____

_____

_____

_____

_____

_____

_____

_____

_____

_____

_____

_____

_____

_____

_____

_____

_____

_____

_____

_____

_____

_____

_____

_____

Day 21 ... Formidable team

"The righteous choose their friends carefully, but the way of the wicked leads them astray" (Proverbs 12:26)

A couple days before I wrote this chapter, my Pastor preached on the theme 'Building a formidable team'. The Cambridge dictionary defines formidable as "Causing you to have fear or respect for something or someone because that thing or person is large, powerful, or difficult".

I found their use of the word fear interesting because it reminded me of 1 Peter 1:17, ***"So you must live in reverent fear of Him during your time here as "temporary residents"***. I am not sure if you realize it but 1 Peter 1:17 is really a charge to us to live in reverent fear of God, not because of what He can do, but because of who He is and what He has done for us.

Anyway, as I meditated on the words formidable and fear, it made me realize that what we need as Christians are friends we 'fear', not because they will hurt us but because they are serious about the things of God. I am talking about friends who will hold us accountable and push us to act right when we are doing wrong. Their support should push us to want to serve God even more.

We need to have an inner circle that causes the devil to tremble when he hears their names. Friends who not only come to us about our behavior but offer solutions as well. Our inner circle should stand ready to apply Galatians 6:1-2 to our lives at all time:

"Dear brothers and sisters, if another believer is overcome by some sin, you who are godly should gently and humbly help that person back onto the right path. And be careful not to fall into the same temptation yourself. Share each other's burdens, and in this way obey the law of Christ."

Just to add, you have to be this type of friend too. Live in such a way that your friends fear you because they know you will not stand for or accept any kind of worldly living in their lives. Be a friend that says. "I see where you are going, but you have to get your act together. I will not stay around and watch you wreck your life. I want the Lord to say well done good and faithful servant when you stand before Him". Some friends will not be receptive. Some will feel threatened as though you are judging them. Do not be daunted by that. Lift them up in prayer and be fervent in your travailing. God will bring them back to where they first saw Him.

- Personal Reflection -

What kind of friends do you have in your inner circle? Take the time to evaluate them. Allow the Lord to guide this process.

Notes

_____

_____

_____

_____

_____

_____

_____

_____

_____

_____

_____

_____

_____

_____

_____

_____

_____

_____

_____

_____

_____

_____

_____

Day 22: Friendship trap

"Jesus turned and said to Peter, "Get behind me, Satan!
You are a stumbling block to me; you do not have in
mind the concerns of God, but merely human concerns"
(Matthew 16:23)

The essence of a Christian friendship is to remind us of who we are and what's most important. A godly friend should help us keep our eyes on God and should never have us place our affection elsewhere. When we are weak, they must be strong.

Still, there will be persons around us, who will act as a hindrance to where we are going. Take for example, Simon Peter. Though Peter had good intentions and cared deeply for Jesus, he was standing in the way of what Jesus had come to earth to fulfil. Matthew 16: 21-23 tells the story of Jesus predicting

His own death and relating this to His disciples about what would happen when He got to Jerusalem. Instead of responding in a way that encouraged Jesus to do His assignment, the NLT Bible says Peter took Jesus aside, reprimanding Him. A reprimand is "an expression of disapproval". In other words, Peter rebuked Jesus' purpose on the earth.

Peter is like many friends and acquaintances we meet along the way. He had no ill will towards Jesus and to the natural eye, it may have appeared that he was just being a genuine friend; one concerned about the suffering Jesus would encounter. Jesus saw it differently, however. Peter was a threat, a way of coming between Him and His obedience to His father. Hence, Jesus rebuked Peter with these words, *"Get away from me Satan, You are a **dangerous trap** for me. You are seeing things merely from a human point of view, not from God's"*.

Jesus recognized that Peter was focused on earthly things. He then had to step in and rebuke the spirit of Satan that was with Peter. Our experiences are likely to be similar. The people we encounter will influence the way we finish in one way or another.

Like Jesus, we will have to recognize when our friends are more bad than good for us. We also need to recognize when the enemy has set a dangerous trap for us. Even if that trap is a friend trap.

Our circle will need to be people who offer encouragement as we pursue our purpose. People who will motivate us to run the race God has set out for us regardless of the circumstances. There is a popular saying "No man is an Island. No man stands alone". Ecclesiastes 4:9 -12 explains the saying in its entirety:

"Two people are better off than one, for they can help each other succeed. If one person falls, the other can reach out and help. But someone who falls alone is in real trouble.

Likewise, two people lying close together can keep each other warm. But how can one be warm alone? A person standing alone can be attacked and defeated, but two can stand back-to-back and conquer. Three are even better, for a triple-braided cord is not easily broken."

Not everyone should be allowed into our inner circle. We need people that are like-minded, who have the same goals. This is important because we need to be able to rely on them to pick us up and point us in the right direction when we fall. In fact, our inner circle should be able to perceive the attacks against us and warn us.

- Personal Reflection -

Are there friends in your inner circle that you need to be wary of? Pray about it and ask God to reveal to you any Simon Peter like traps you will need to avoid?

Notes

_____

_____

_____

_____

_____

_____

_____

_____

_____

_____

_____

_____

_____

_____

_____

_____

_____

_____

_____

_____

_____

_____

_____

_____

Day 23 ... God desires a repentant heart

"I have had one message for the Jews and Greeks alike - the necessity of repenting from sin and turning to God, and of having faith in our Lord Jesus"
(Acts 20:21)

Each Christian is a target of the devil. This is because he wants to destroy us, and the promises of God for us (John 10:10). One of the goals the devil has set for us is for us to fall (falter) because he knows when we fall, grace will be the furthest thing from our minds. A fall from grace will cause some of us to bathe in self-pity and disappointment, refusing to carry out our journey to the end. The devil knows we may feel as though we have failed God and are no longer worthy of Him.

Though we may fail, we each must believe we can complete the race and win. We must have faith that this victory will cause us to enter through the pearly gates and hear the words *"well done my good and faithful servant"* (Matthew 25:21, NIV). However, it requires that we have faith, believing God is with us and will never leave nor forsake us (Deuteronomy 31:6). That no matter how many times we fall, like David, He wants us to have a heart that will be repentant. This is why David writes, *"a broken and a contrite heart, O God, thou wilt not despise"* (Psalm 51:17b, KJV).

If you are one who turns away from God when you fall because of self-pity, shame, self-condemnation etc., say the prayer below and ask God for the strength to get back up no matter how many times you may falter.

Prayer: "Father I believe Your Word that says you will never leave me nor forsake me. Lord help me to get back up when I fall, and like David, to believe that You want a relationship with me no matter how often I fail you. Help me to understand how much you love me despite my weaknesses and failures. Strengthen me O God. Amen."

- *Personal Reflection* -

Write a list of the areas you tend to falter in then ask God why you keep faltering. Then, one by one, declare aloud that you surrender the area and the reason for it to God. For example, if the area you tend to falter in is lying and the reason for that is fear of failure then, you would declare:

"Lord I surrender this habit of lying to you. I know I do it because of my fear of failing and I surrender that fear to you as well."

Notes

_____

_____

_____

_____

_____

_____

_____

_____

_____

_____

_____

_____

_____

_____

_____

_____

_____

_____

_____

_____

_____

_____

_____

_____

_____

_____

_____

Day 24...The athlete

*"But we are citizens of heaven, where the Lord Jesus
Christ lives. And we are eagerly waiting for him to return
as our Savior" (Philippians 3:20)*

W hen a professional athlete has an upcoming race, that athlete ensures he goes through adequate and rigorous training, especially if his goal is not just to take part, but to **WIN.** That athlete will monitor his weaknesses and will work assiduously to correct these, by practicing and taking precautions so he may be in tiptop form once the race comes around. He will attempt to do everything necessary to achieve the goal he has set for himself.

The difference between the race the athlete runs and the race we run as Christians is that our race is not for the swift, but for those who can endure. Although this is the case, our race requires the same effort that an athlete would spend. We have to give ourselves daily to remembering and reinforcing our goal in this life because if we take our eyes off the goal, we will lose the prize at the end of the race. Paul wrote, *"Do you not know that in a race all the runners run, but only one gets the prize? Run in such a way as to get the prize. Everyone who competes in the games goes into strict training"* (1 Corinthians 9:24-25)

I think some Christians have become too comfortable in this race not realizing that it is not a destination but a journey. One we must endure until the end. We have to say like Paul that we count what we have left behind as garbage so we can gain Christ and be one with Him. Like Paul when people see us, they should see a difference. Paul stood out among thousands of people because he insisted that those among him would know where he stood in this life. He wanted to be on the right side of God. He wanted to ensure that when the Lord judges the world, he would be right in the sight of God. And just like Paul, we too should bear at all times in our minds that Jesus is coming again and we must be ready to meet Him in Glory, having lived a life that pleases Him. John in Matthew 3: 8 writes *"Prove by the way you live that*

you have repented of your sins and turned to God".
What does this mean for us? It means that our lives
must reflect Christ (not conformed to this world, but
eating, sleeping, and breathing the ways of our
Heavenly Father).

*"For our citizenship is in heaven, from which also we
eagerly wait for a Savior, the Lord Jesus Christ"
(Philippians 3:20).*

- Personal Reflection -

What are some of the things that you will need to do
to ensure that you start and/or remain in strict training,
pressing on towards your eternal goal?

Notes

_____
_____
_____
_____
_____
_____
_____
_____
_____
_____
_____
_____
_____
_____
_____
_____
_____
_____
_____
_____
_____
_____
_____
_____

Day 25 ... Keep pressing

"I press toward the mark for the prize of the high calling of God in Christ Jesus" (Philippians 3:14)

K eep pressing! Even when it is not easy. It was not easy for Christ to die for us but He did it because He loves us and wants us to get back to a place where we have a direct relationship with the Father. It is not easy at all but it is worth it.

I will be honest. Sometimes I wanted to give up on this Christianity thing. I wanted to enjoy my university years. I wanted to party and do all the things young adults do and I remember one day saying to God, "I will live my life, and when I am ready I will come back to you". However, the Lord gently replied, "The day you step out there may be your last. You would have spent your time as a Christian being a testimony to persons and they will make it in but you will not." I knew this meant that being a Christian was not to be taken lightly. Therefore, I started to be even more deliberate about remaining steadfast and not falling to sin. However, as soon as I do, I repent and ask God for His forgiveness. I came to realize that it is important to embrace the love and grace of God and not take it for granted.

Some people do not understand why I am the way I am. In addition, because they do not understand, they say and do hateful things. Their ultimate aim - to get me to turn away from God. Maybe you have experienced similar things in your Christian walk. I empathize with you if you have. The truth is the Bible tells us to expect persecution. Our only choice as Christians even in the times of persecution is to **STAND BOLDLY.**

In the meantime, do not be afraid to take your concerns to God. If you feel you are about to give up on God then take it to the Lord in prayer. Cry out before Him. Ask Him to cleanse you and make you whole. Ask Him to take you back to the place where you first received Him.

Do not run from God when you feel like giving up. Run to him! Draw close to Him and His Word, and as He has promised, He will draw close to you. Make it a duty to just be real with God. Tell Him as it is.

- Think on this -

People are coming out of the closet. They are boldly exhibiting their lifestyles. We need to do so as Christians too. We need to let the world know who we are. **We must do what is necessary to overpower their darkness!**

Remember no matter how dark a room is, as long as light is placed in that room the people in that room will see the light. As Christians, we need to **be the light, regardless of the darkness around us** so that others may come to know and want to pursue the things of God.

Notes

_____

_____

_____

_____

_____

_____

_____

_____

_____

_____

_____

_____

_____

_____

_____

_____

_____

_____

_____

_____

_____

_____

_____

_____

Day 26 ...
Thanksgiving

Today is not a day of teaching. Instead, today it is a day of thanksgiving. Today I want you to use the first musical instrument ever made (your mouth) to give thanks and praise unto to God for who He is.

The scripture below will be your golden text for today.

> *"I will praise you, Lord my God, with all my heart; I will glorify your name forever"* (Psalms 86:12)

Meditate on the song, Glory to the Lamb by Geoffrey Golden, and journal as the Lord shares His thoughts with you.

Notes

_____

_____

_____

_____

_____

_____

_____

_____

_____

_____

_____

_____

_____

_____

_____

_____

_____

_____

_____

_____

_____

_____

_____

_____

_____

Day 27…Prayer

Today I want you to declare that going forward you are going to spend at least five (5) minutes every day communicating with God. Not necessarily asking Him for anything but just to let Him know how you are feeling and how your day was.

Having an active prayer life is important because it is a command. The apostle Paul states that we should not worry about anything but instead we should pray about everything (Philippians 4:6-7). Luke 18:1 states *"Then Jesus told his disciples a parable to show them that they should always pray and not give up"*.

We talk with our friends daily, let us ensure that Jesus is on the list of persons we spend time with in conversation.

- Personal Reflection -

How would you describe your prayer life with God? Would you say you prioritize Him, the way you priotize family and friends? If no, journal what changes you will make going forward.

Notes

_____

_____

_____

_____

_____

_____

_____

_____

_____

_____

_____

_____

_____

_____

_____

_____

_____

Day 28 ... Spread the Gospel

"And He said to them, 'Go into all the world and preach the gospel to every creature". (Mark 16:15)

Today I want you to find persons that are unsaved and spread the Good News of Christ with them. Ask the Lord to reveal to you persons who need to hear of His love for them. When you are done, I want you to make a note of them including their names. Then, in your prayer time, I want you to pray for them to commit to God as Lord and Savior and to activate the call of God on their lives. Remember allow the Lord to guide this process. Go make a Disciple!

Notes

_____

_____

_____

_____

_____

_____

_____

_____

_____

_____

_____

_____

_____

_____

_____

_____

_____

Day 29...Reflection

Make a note of all that you have learnt while reading this devotional.

Notes

_____
_____
_____
_____
_____
_____
_____
_____
_____
_____
_____
_____
_____
_____
_____
_____
_____

C o n c l u s i o n

I admit. Nothing I have written in this book is as easy as 1-2-3. I know resisting temptation can sometimes be hard. Loving others and forgiving anyone that has hurt us is hard. Despite how hard it may be, we *can do all things through Christ who strengthens us!* After all that is what Paul said. He realized that it was possible to live as God commanded. He also knew that by himself he could do nothing. He knew he needed Jesus.

Research states it takes approximately 21 days to break into habit. If we want our godly response to become a habit, we will need to practice our godly response and call on Jesus every time we feel like throwing in the towel! It means we will need to have Scriptures that we rely on for every area of our lives!

Whenever we get out of line with what makes God happy we need to study, pray and fast about it. We must pray without ceasing! Before we start our day, we ought to say, "Lord not my will but thine be done, let the words of my mouth and the mediation of my heart be acceptable in your sight, let me be conscious about my heavenly prize today as you order my steps in your Word!" We should also repent before bed. I mean put down the phone, go to our secret place and repent before God, asking Him to forgive us and purge us from all our fleshly desires.

Let us be good soil Christians who hear the word of God and apply it. Let us be "rooted and grounded in the name of the Lord." Let us above all else be 'Ready for His Return'!

*"And why should we ourselves risk our lives hour by hour? For I swear, dear brothers and sisters, that I face death daily. This is as certain as my pride in what Christ Jesus our Lord has done in you. And what value was there in fighting wild beasts—those people of Ephesus—if there will be no resurrection from the dead? And if there is no resurrection, "Let's feast and drink, for tomorrow we die!" Don't be fooled by those who say such things, for **"bad company corrupts good character."** Think carefully about what is right, and stop sinning. For to your shame I say that some of you don't know God at all".*

(1 Corinthians 15: 30-34)

About the Author

Ashley is a people person and loves to offer words of encouragement to anyone in need. She is a recent university graduate and holds a Bachelor in Marketing and Operations Management.

Above all, Ashley is a sold out child of God. Her favorite scripture is "But as for me and my house, we will serve the Lord" (Joshua 24:15, NKJV). She boldly proclaims it since for her it has to be Jesus all the way!

Ashley has a passion for other young women. She wants to see them live and find their identity in Christ and Christ alone. She truly wants to see them discipled for the Kingdom of God!

Thanks for reading!